Little Bear and Emily

A QUARREL

A story of friendship ...

Text by Florence Ducatteau
Illustrated by Chantal Peten

PLURUS

Oliver and Emily like to play almost every day.

They find lots of snails in the grass. 'Look at this one! It is huge!'
says Oliver.

They play hide and seek. 'eight, nine, ten, I'm coming,' shouts Oliver.

'Mmmm… This is wonderful. The air smells fresh and the view is so beautiful. I really like it here, don't you?' says Emily.

The two friends play leap frog over each other. 'Now it's your turn, Emily,' says Oliver.

'Let's play tea parties?' says Emily.
Oliver stops and frowns. 'What! Tea Parties?'

'I don't want to play tea parties. That's a stupid game
for girls,' says Oliver.
'It's not just for girls and it is not stupid,' says Emily.
'Boys can play it, too.'

The two playmates aren't speaking and they are no longer playing together either. They ignore each other.

'If she thinks I am going to play that silly game she had better think again!' says Oliver.

'If he thinks he can stop me playing this game he had better think again,' says Emily.

'I don't care. I will play a game on my own. Who needs her?'

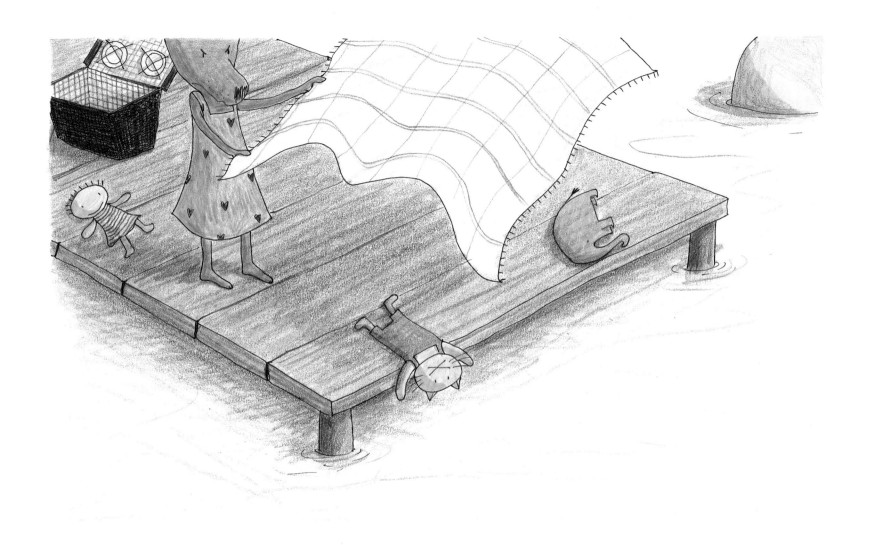

'I can still play tea parties on my own. I don't need him.'

'I know. I shall build a raft and sail it on the river. Max can be the captain,' says Oliver.

'Would you like some tea, little elephant?How about some biscuits
for you too?' asks Emily.

'I wonder what Emily is doing now?' says Oliver, sadly.

'I wonder what Oliver is doing now?' asks Emily, tearfully.

'Oh, no. My raft has broken free from the string. Help, it is going to crash on the rocks. Poor Max will get very wet.'

'Oh, no ! Max is in danger on the raft. I must try and help him.'

'Come on, Max, I've got you. Phew, that was close!' says Emily.
'Have you managed to catch him Emily?'
'Yes, I have, Oliver. He's safe again, now.'

'Phew, thank you, Emily. I was so worried.
Look. I'm really sorry about earlier.'
'So am I, Oliver,' says Emily.

'Let's have a snail race using some paper boats I have made?'
suggests Oliver.